*For Gaëlle and
for Jacques*

First published 1997 by Kaléidoscope,
France, under the title *Léon et Albertine*

This edition published 2000 by Walker Books Ltd
87 Vauxhall Walk, London SE11 5HJ

2 4 6 8 10 9 7 5 3 1

© 1997 Kaléidoscope
Translation © 1999 Walker Books Ltd

This book has been typeset in New Baskerville.

Printed in France

British Library Cataloguing in Publication Data
A catalogue record for this book is
available from the British Library.

ISBN 0-7445-7731-4

THIS WALKER BOOK BELONGS TO:

_____

_____

_____

_____

Frankie and Albertine

Christine Davenier

WALKER BOOKS
AND SUBSIDIARIES

LONDON • BOSTON • SYDNEY

Frankie the pig had never felt so low.
He had fallen in love.

Albertine was the hen of his dreams –
but she had never even noticed him!
What shall I do?
Frankie wondered.

He decided to ask
his friends.

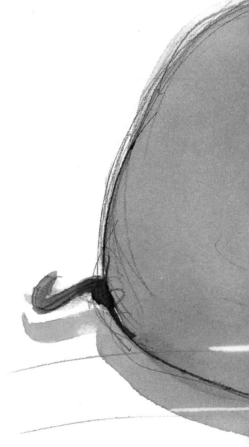

"Cu

ck-a-doodle
-doo!

"… Sing to her, Frankie!"
said Rooster. "The best
way to get a hen's
attention is to sing!"

But Albertine snored
through Frankie's
song.

"Dance for her, Frankie!" called out
Rabbit. "That's the best way
to tell her how you feel!"

But Albertine was having her lunch,
and never even looked up.

"Strut your stuff, Frankie!" said Turkey. "That's the best way to woo a hen!"

But Albertine was too busy
to notice.

"Be bold, Frankie!" snorted Bull. "Show her how strong you are. That's the best way!"

But Albertine paid no attention at all.

"I know!" said Duck. "Do a super-duper duck dive. That's the best way to show Albertine how you feel!"

Whoops!

It's no use, thought Frankie. *Albertine will never, ever notice me.* And he shuffled off to hide his tears.

"Hey, Frankie!" called his friend Gus. "Don't go away. Come and play with me!"

Well ... why not? thought Frankie.
He jumped in the puddle and
the two pigs splashed and
sang and laughed so much
that Frankie forgot
to be sad.

Frankie's happy squeals
sounded across the farmyard,
and soon everyone was tumbling
about in the mud.

Suddenly, Frankie looked up
and there she was, smiling at him:
Albertine, the hen of his dreams.

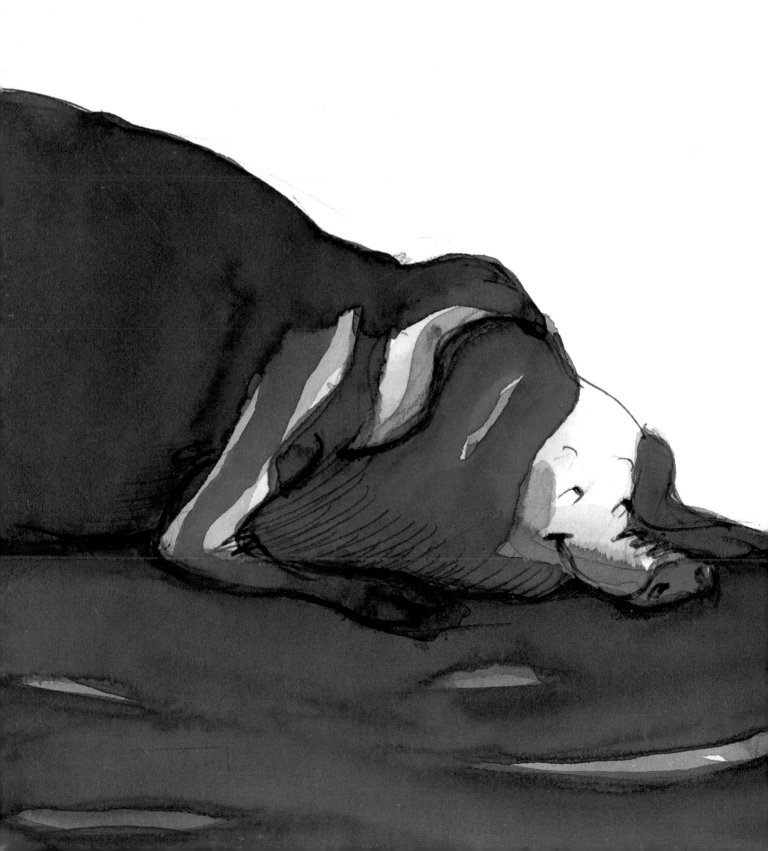

"Oh, Frankie!" she said. "What fun you are! Let's do it again."

Frankie closed his eyes.
He took a deep, deep breath.
And then, without asking anyone
what to do, Frankie whispered,
"I love you, Albertine!"

WALKER 🐻 BOOKS

Frankie and Albertine

CHRISTINE DAVENIER says that first and foremost *Frankie and Albertine* is "a love story". The theme is "just be yourself and don't try to act as you think others expect you to act". She deliberately chose animals with very different shapes – a big awkward pig and a small lively hen. "When I draw," she reveals, "my face and my body take the expression and attitude of my characters. For this story, I really enjoyed imagining myself as a pig dancing and also as the hen the pig was trying to seduce!"

Christine Davenier has illustrated several children's books, including *Very Best (Almost) Friends*, a book of poems collected by Paul B. Janeczko, and her own story *Sleepy Sophie*. Christine is French and lives in Paris.

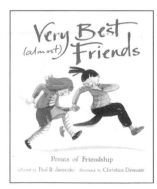

ISBN 0-7445-5617-1 (hb)

ISBN 0-7445-7503-6 (hb)